To the childre~ ...

Hope you en

CH00847144

PHILLIP FLOP'S

top 10 fails

DAVE BURROWS

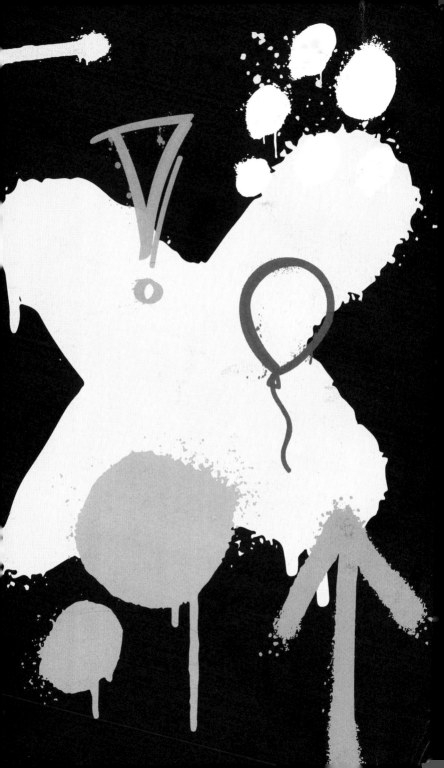

a pork → chopper

FLYING PIG BOOKS

FP

Copyright Dave Burrows 2021

Stare at
this spot for
5 seconds
EXACTLY.

No reason, I just
wanted to see if
you would.

My name is Phillip Flop. Yes, I know it's a ridiculous name and it sounds like Flip Flop. I've been told that a BAZILLION times. It's a long story involving my dad and his terrible sense of humour. Actually, it's a pretty short one - he called me it because he thought it was funny. Well, I've got news for you...

1

IT ISN'T

Anyway, I've been keeping a diary recently and I realised that quite a few things in my life don't exactly go to plan and that someone might find these funny. I certainly didn't at the time but looking back I guess... maybe.

NUMBER 10

THE SMOOTHIE INCIDENT

We were having a lesson at school a couple of months back when our teacher, Mr King, was talking about healthy eating. He was saying that you should eat a lot of fruit and that apparently chocolate oranges don't count. Then he said that a good way of eating enough fruit was to mix it up into a smoothie so we looked at some recipes using bananas, apples, strawberries, pineapples and all sorts.

I'm not that into fruit but they did look pretty tasty. After that we watched a video about how to make one and then we wrote up into our books what sort of smoothie we would like to make.

When I got home I couldn't wait to give it a go. My mum was in the kitchen, cleaning. I told her about the smoothie thing and I could tell she wasn't really listening but she said,

"Okay then, just DON'T MAKE A MESS!"

I remembered seeing a blender at the back of one of the kitchen cupboards that hadn't been used for ages. I dug out loads of stuff from the cupboard and sure enough there it was, covered in dust.

I blew it off, plugged it in then grabbed a load of fruit and rammed it in all the way to the top, then I poured some milk in. Pretty sure that I'd remembered everything, I switched it on.

Then I realised that I hadn't remembered everything...

THE LID!

I was ABSOLUTELY COVERED, head to foot, in smoothie juice. My mum came in to see what all the noise was about and, let's just say, wasn't very pleased -

"PHILLIP! I'VE JUST CLEANED THIS AND YOU'VE GOT IT EVERYWHERE, INCLUDING THE CEILING! YOU NEED TO CLEAN THIS UP, NOW!!!"

The walls were covered in strawberries, the door in pineapple and the floor banana. I was thinking it was going to take aaaaaaaaaages to clean up when Ned, our dog, also came to have a look at what was going on.

He couldn't believe his luck and straight away started licking it up (The door was his favourite). It gave me a great idea. I lay on the floor and let him lick me all over. It felt pretty funny but he did quite a good job.

Unfortunately, he couldn't reach the ceiling!

SLURRP

BEFORE:

AFTER:

NUMBER 9

THE GARDENING INCIDENT

A while ago Dad was doing some gardening when he asked me if I wanted to earn some money. He needed me to pick up all of the leaves in the back garden so that he could mow the grass. It sounded like a pretty dull job but I agreed because he said he'd give me £5!

There were LOADS of leaves though. It was November so they had all fallen off the trees and had started to go really slimy. I was picking them up with my bare hands but they felt horrible and it was taking ages.

I filled 2 big bags full of them and still hadn't even put a dent in it. Then I found some gloves which was a bit better but it was still taking too long.

I decided that I needed a plan so I headed back into the house to watch some TV, which is where I do my best thinking. Dad said that if I wasn't done in 1 hour then I wouldn't get paid so I had to think of a plan and fast.

This is what I came up with, together with some small problems:

1) Hide the leaves somewhere. (Where, I didn't know.)

2) Paint them green so you couldn't see them. (The problem being I didn't have any green paint and it would probably take longer than actually picking them up.)

3) Get Ned to do it by hiding some dog treats under the leaves. (He'd probably make more of a mess finding them).

So, none of these would really work. Then it hit me. It was right in front of my face! My mum's new vacuum cleaner! It was (apparently) a new, top of the range thing that would suck up anything.

I thought I'd be doing my mum a favour by testing it out by sucking up a huge pile of soggy leaves. I took it out into the back garden without anyone noticing and fired it up. It was working pretty well and doing a good job with the leaves. I was getting some pretty funny looks from the neighbours but I didn't care if it was going to get the job done nice and quick.

After a few minutes I could smell something, like a burning smell. Then I noticed smoke coming from the vacuum cleaner. I kind of panicked a bit. Just then mum came outside so I quickly stood in front of it and tried to act casual.

When she'd gone I snuck it back inside and put it back in the exact position that I found it, so that she would have no idea that I'd used it.

Somehow she did.

My mum is smarter than she looks.

NUMBER 8
{ HIDE AND SEEK }

We were doing a PE lesson recently, when Mr King took us to the field and said, "We're going to play hide and seek. I'm going to give everyone 2 minutes to find a good hiding place and then I will come to find you. As soon as I find someone they will become a seeker and they will help me to find the others, okay?"

Sounded fair enough, and I had thought of THE BEST hiding place!

Only me, Freya and Ali (my best friends) knew about it. We made sure no one was looking and made straight for it.

Basically, there is a fence running all the way around the edge of the field with a thick hedge behind it.

A small bit of the fence is broken and there is a hole dug out underneath the hedge just big enough to get 3 small 9 year olds in!

in here

We lay down and were dead quiet. We could hear people being found and running around looking for others. After a while it all went quiet like the game had finished. We weren't falling for that trick though. As soon as we jumped out everyone would appear and scream, "FOUND YOU!". So, we carried on being silent.

It got a bit boring after a while so we played 'eye spy'. But, seeing as we were inside a bush there wasn't much to see.

None of us were wearing a watch but it felt like we had been there quite a while and we were starting to get hungry.

My stomach was growling like an angry badger.

We thought it was probably about 9.30 but then we saw the infants coming out to play which meant it was actually 11 o'clock! We quickly scampered out of our hiding place and ran back to class, covered in dirt. We peeked through the window and could see they were in the middle of a maths test.

We did a quick game of rock, paper, scissors to see who would have the short straw of opening the door. Freya lost, so I did the gentlemanly thing of letting her go in first.

Mr King was shocked and pretty annoyed.

"Where on earth have you three been?" he asked.

"Erm, hiding," we said as one.

"What do we win???"

"A detention," was the reply.

NUMBER 7

WORLD BOOK DAY

- - - - - - - - - - - -

World Book Day happens every year in April. I'm sure you do something for it in your school. At my school (Griswold Junior) we always dress up as our favourite book character and prizes are given for the best ones so some people go to quite a bit of effort.

It's really funny seeing the teachers wearing weird outfits. I remember World Book Day last year, Mr King was telling Ryan Evans off for eating wax crayons.

my favourite are the red ones - they taste of strawberries

Ryan would've normally been really scared by this but it's pretty hard to take someone seriously when they're dressed as an Oompa Loompa so Ryan was just laughing his head off.

So far I've done Woody from Toy Story (a cowboy) and Fantastic Mr Fox but this year I decided to try something a bit different. I spent ages planning it and it took even longer to put together.

You know 'The Very Hungry Caterpillar', right? Well, that is Lily's (Lily is my little sister) favourite book so I decided to go as that. My mum spent days sewing it together and when it was finished the outfit was REALLY long and trailed behind me so I looked like a proper caterpillar and everything.

On the way to school we bumped into one of the kids from the year below who I sort of know. Strangely, he wasn't wearing an outfit but I just figured he couldn't find one or had forgot or something.

Then, as I turned into the playground I noticed everyone, and I mean everyone, in their regular royal blue Griswold Junior School jumpers. I couldn't believe it.

My mum searched on her phone - When is World Book Day? The answer - NEXT Wednesday!

"Well, we haven't got time to go home and get you changed so you're just going to have to wear that I'm afraid. I think you look great!" my mum said as she disappeared sharpish.

So I had to sit in lessons ALL DAY dressed as a caterpillar. I couldn't even take it off because I was only wearing a vest and pants underneath and that would've been even worse.

Mr King told me to go and look in the lost property box for spare uniform but all I found in there was a skirt for a 4 year old girl, one PE pump, a school tie that looked like it was from about 1985 and a few jelly babies covered in fluff.

So, I just had to style it out. Or at least try to anyway. Oh, and the jelly babies were actually quite nice.

NUMBER 6

WORLD BOOK DAY. PART 2

So, a week after this happened and it really was World Book Day, guess what happened?

That's right. I forgot.

So I was the ONLY person NOT in a costume!

NUMBER 5
SCHOOL PHOTO DAY

We had the school photographer in a couple of months ago. Mum really looks forwards to it every year and goes a bit crazy with making sure we look smart.

She washes all the uniforms the night before, irons them and hangs them up then she makes us have a bath, wash our hair and scrub ourselves all over including all the dirt between my toes and in my ears and everything.

Then we have to go to bed extra early so we don't look tired in the photograph. Then she gets us up super early (?!) so she can get us ready.

I'm a bit of a messy eater so she won't let me put my uniform on until I've eaten my breakfast, so I'm sat there eating my crackle pops in my pants, feeling like a complete doofus.

When I've had my breakfast, washed my face, brushed my teeth, combed my hair and washed my face again THEN I'm allowed to put my uniform on. It was raining outside so I had to put my waterproof coat on and my mum grabbed a big umbrella.

"Now, I've polished your shoes so DON'T PLAY FOOTBALL in them before the photograph!" she said to me as we headed out of the door.

This is the word that I didn't hear

(DON'T) PLAY FOOTBALL IN THEM BEFORE THE PHOTOGRAPH!

When we got to the school gate she knelt down next to me, she straightened my tie, redid my shoelaces, brushed my hair, pulled my trousers up and then licked a handkerchief and wiped it all over my face.

Oh, and did I mention that EVERYONE was watching this?

She is so embarrassing. Then she said, "You look like a right Bobby Dazzler, I can't wait to see the photograph. Have a super day. DON'T get dirty."

I've got no idea who Bobby Dazzler is either.

My mum turned away and I headed across the playground. I knew I was going to have to be super careful.

The photographs weren't till after lunch so I was going to have to be on guard all day. 5 seconds later a ball rolled towards me from the other side of the playground. I couldn't help it, my foot just kind of took over and booted the ball back where it came from, leaving a big muddy mark all over my shiny shoes.

I headed inside and went to the bathroom where I cleaned it off as well as I could, then went to class.

Everything was fine until breaktime. I told Ali and Freya that I couldn't play football, as much as I wanted to, so I was playing catch with some of my other friends.

Max threw the ball to me and it sailed way over my head and landed in a bush. I reached up for it but couldn't get close enough so had to go right into the bush, it was then that I realised it was a holly bush and was REALLY prickly.

My uniform kept getting caught and I had to yank it hard to pull it free. I'd nearly got the ball so I stretched up as far and I could and just about wrapped my fingers around it.

I pulled it towards me and it came free, but as it did the branch that it was resting on sprung back and whacked me in the face. I climbed out of the bush and everyone screamed. "Oh my god, did you get attacked in there? You're covered in blood, you look like you've been savaged by an especially angry cat."

AN ANGRY CAT

Is this Turkey and Rabbit flavour because I specifically asked for Duck and Pheasant

TIDDLES

I ran back to the toilets to check the damage. It wasn't great, as well as the blood on my face my clothes were covered in small holes. I grabbed a paper towel and tried to clean the blood off my face but it kind of just wiped it around.

Later on in the afternoon, it was time for the photograph. We were told to be ready in 5 minutes so there was just enough time for one final visit to the bathroom (I'd spent more time in there than the classroom) to check that my hair looked okay.

I could see a bit of it sticking up so I just got a little bit of water from the tap and pushed it down. It stayed down for about 3 seconds and then sprang back up, so I used a bit more water.

Long story short, a few minutes later I was stood in the bathroom with a soaking wet head. It was dripping all over the place. I shoved my head under the hand dryer but I only had time to do half of my hair before Mr King sent Ali to come and get me.

The photo came back a couple of weeks later...

FLOP. P

At first Mum was pretty angry that she couldn't just have a 'nice, normal photo' of me. But then she started laughing and didn't stop for about an hour. Then she bought one for EVERY relative that I have!

GRANDMA

UNCLE MARVIN

AUNTY LOU

COUSIN WENDY

← COUSINS WHOSE NAMES I CAN'T REMEMBER

UNCLE PETE

← UNCLE PETE'S NEIGHBOUR (not even a relative)

UNCLE PETE'S NEIGHBOUR'S CAT (not even human)

NUMBER 4

MILKSHAKE

When I was about 5 I was quite into farm animals. One day my annoying older brother, Billy, came into my bedroom and said, "I've got a BRILLIANT fact about cows, but I'm not telling you it."

This made me want to REALLY know it so I bugged him for ages.

Finally he said, "Okay then, I'll tell you. But I'm feeling a bit peckish, go and get me some of those chocolates out of the kitchen."

"The posh ones we're not allowed?" I replied.

"Yeh, those ones," he said.

So, I had to creep downstairs and quietly open the kitchen door without anyone noticing. Dad was watching the TV so that wasn't really a problem but Ned was a different matter. He can hear when you open the treats cupboard even if he's at the bottom of the garden. He would probably hear it if he was on the other side of the world, and asleep.

I opened the door as slowly as possible and straight away he was woofing his head off.

"NED, BE QUIET!" shouted my dad.

"I need to see who wins 'Masked Celebrities Dancing and Singing on Ice in a Jungle Factor'."

So, with a handful of chocolates, I shot back upstairs.

Billy took them and said, "Right then, the big fact. The big, secret fact. You know that milk comes from cows, right?"

I nodded.

"Well, you know if you milk a regular cow, and by regular I mean mostly a white colour?"

"Yehhhhhh," I said.

"Well, milk that white cow and you get normal milk out of it but if you were to find a brown cow and milk it then you would get chocolate milk!"

I was amazed. "Really??????????????"

"Absolutely, yeh. And that's not even the best bit. There is a rare type of cow that is a golden colour. Hardly anyone has ever seen one. You know that cows have 4 udders don't you, the bits under the cow that the milk comes from? Well, if you find a golden cow and you milk it then one udder makes vanilla flavour milk, one of them makes chocolate, the next banana and the last one strawberry!"

It was too much to take. My head nearly exploded.

BANG

And so, when my class visited the children's farm a few weeks after I couldn't wait to share it.

EVERYONE laughed their boots off.

THE LESSER SPOTTED GOLDEN COW

VANILLA

STRAWBERRY

CHOCOLATE

BANANA

NUMBER 3

BIKE RACE

Ali came over on his bike a few weeks ago. We were going to time each other racing around the block to see if we could beat our best ever time (3mins 24secs). We take it VERY seriously, we've got a spreadsheet and everything.

This led to Ali and me making some changes to our bikes to make them as fast as possible. I started taking bits off to make it lighter, which kind of worked. There are a few things that you don't really need like water bottles etc.

I took the saddle out too because I figured I was standing up most of the time anyway. This made me a good few seconds lighter around the block so I started removing more and more things.

We got a bit carried away because I ended up with basically just a frame - no gears, no brakes, no chain and no wheels! (It was very light though.)

Once I'd put it all back together I had a few bits left over. I hoped that these bits wouldn't be too important. The bike hasn't fallen apart since so I'm guessing they weren't. Anyway, Ali got to mine and then realised that he'd got a puncture. He didn't have a clue how to fix one and said that when it happens he normally just buys a new bike.

I told him, "No problem, I've got this. 100%, I've seen my dad do this loads of times."

Ali seemed really impressed, "Wow, really? You can fix this?"

"Absolutely." I lied.

The thing was I had seen my dad do it before but I had never actually done it myself.

I knew that the first thing that you needed to do was to take the wheel off which we actually managed to do quite easily.

Then the difficult bit was taking the tyre off the wheel. Dad used tyre lever things before but I couldn't find any of those.

I went searching in the house for something else to use. I struck gold in the cutlery drawer with a few of my mum's best spoons.

I wedged them between the tyre and the wheel rim and gave them a pull. After a few goes the tyre popped off.

The spoons got a little bit bent so I tried to bend them back and they kind of snapped. I say kind of I mean totally and completely. I just hoped my mum wouldn't notice that the spoons had got shorter since she last used them. I'd just have to say,

"I don't know Mum, maybe your hands have got bigger?"

Then we had to pull the inner tube out and find out where the hole was. I remembered this bit - all you need to do is pump some air into it and then hold it against your face and feel for the air coming out. Or you can put it in a bucket of water and you'll see bubbles coming out of the hole! Then you mark where the hole is so you don't lose it again.

After that you just stick a little patch over the hole with some special glue, stick it back into the tyre, reattach the wheel and you're good to go. Sounds easy doesn't it?

4 and a half hours later I was pretty pleased with the job. The tyre was pumped up and we were ready to race. There was only one problem...

It had gone dark.

On your marks, get set, GO!

Go where? I can't see my hand in front of my face

Where are you?

★ ★ CRASHHHHHHHH ★ ★ ★

OOOOOOOOOOF!

Oh, they you are

NUMBER 2

BROWNBEARD

This one is down to my no good brother as well - I'd been learning about pirates at school and I thought Blackbeard sounded really cool. He was born in 1680, which I think makes him even older than my grandma. He was pretty mad and everyone was really scared of him. He used to sail around the Caribbean Sea on his ship looking for other ships to steal from.

Anyway, I decided that I wanted to be a pirate and the first thing that I needed to do was to grow a beard.

This is how I imagined I'd look...

I asked my dad about it first because he'd started to grow a beard a while ago because he thought it made him look 'cool'. It didn't. The only reason he wanted to grow one is because he is as bald as a snooker ball and had forgotten what hair felt like.

my dad's shiny head

I was sure I'd be able to pull one off much better though.

Billy must've heard us talking because he told me that he'd got a 'sure fire way of growing a full beard in less than 24 hours, guaranteed.' He sounded like one of the shopping channel presenters that my mum watches, but I was sucked in by his confidence.

He told me about a special mixture that you can spread on your face, leave overnight and you'll wake up with a big beard. The first thing that he said I'd need to collect was some soil which I thought sounded pretty weird.

Billy could tell I wasn't sure so he showed me his laptop and said,

"LOOK, HERE IT IS ON HOWTOGROWABEARDFAST.CO.UK."

Sure enough, there it was in black and white. He read it out, "All you need is a little squirt of shampoo, some moisturiser, a 1kg bag of flour, a mashed up banana, a spoonful of peanut butter, a crumbled up digestive biscuit, a handful of soil and a single feather from a pigeon.

"All you have to do is mash it up together then spread it all over your face and leave it on as you sleep. In the morning you wash if off and hey presto! A fully grown beard!"

I knew this would take some doing. Most of the stuff I could get out of the bathroom or kitchen cupboards so I went and grabbed everything that I could get my hands on. The toughest one was the pigeon feather.

Pigeons are ALWAYS around and bugging you when you don't want them to. I remember one of my favourite games when I was younger (it was last week really...) was 'chase the pigeon' but when you want to find one they just completely disappear.

I eventually found a couple and ran after them. They perched on a branch of the tallest tree in the whole park just to make it extra difficult for me.

Long story short, I fell out of the tree, twice. I was in the tree for a good hour, whenever I even got close to a pigeon it would tilt its head to look at me and then 'pooof' it would be gone. Eventually I gave up.

I jumped down from the tree and what did I land right next to? You guessed it (unless you didn't) a pigeon feather!

So, I had all of the ingredients and I raced home to mix them all together. I locked the bathroom door and got busy mixing in the sink. I'll be honest I did make quite a bit of a mess but these things have got to be done. After a few minutes I'd got a brown, sludgy, foamy and slightly feathery kind of lotion type thing.

I needed something to put it in. I hunted around the bathroom and found one of mum's perfume bottles, it was nearly half empty anyway so I tipped it down the toilet and started shoving the mixture into the bottle with my hands. I hid the bottle in my bedroom until later.

Just before bedtime I emptied the entire bottle all over my face and rubbed it in. It was pretty disgusting but I kept thinking about the beard and how it was going to be totally worth it.

I got into bed and was asleep within seconds, turns out that falling out of trees is tiring work. As the sun rose the next morning, I slowly opened my eyes, or at least tried to. A weird, hard crust had formed all over my face and it was holding my eyes shut tight.

My face was also kind of stuck to my pillow. I put my hands out in front of me and felt my way out of the bedroom and into the bathroom, praying that no one would see me on the way.

I splashed a bit of water around and the pillow slowly started to peel away. I felt a rush of excitement as I thought of all the great things that I'd be able to do with my beard. I'd be able to scare people, pretend to be an adult and even store bits of food in my face.

As I scraped away the layers of muck I felt around for signs of my new face fuzz. But as my fingers ran over my face all I could feel was my bare cheek. There was not a single hair to be seen anywhere!

I couldn't believe it! I ran down into the kitchen to shout at Billy but as soon as my mum saw me she started screaming.

I tried to explain it to her but she didn't get it. She was super annoyed about the pillow, which she threw in the bin. She was super, super, super, super, super, super, super annoyed about the perfume!

Oh, and the website... I checked the name at the bottom of the screen...

HOW TO GROW A BEARD FOR 9 YEAR OLDS

created by Billy Flop.

A few days later I got home from school a couple of minutes early. I really needed the toilet so I ran up the stairs 2 steps at a time and bounded through the bathroom door.

I got a bit of a shock when I saw my dad with the lotion spread all over the top of his head. To be fair, he was pretty surprised too. To start off with he denied all knowledge of his head being covered in the mixture, then he said it was an 'accident' and that he had slipped. Eventually he admitted it and said,

"Well, it was worth a try wasn't it?"

NUMBER 1

BONKERS FOR CONKERS

So then, we've arrived at number 1 - The best/worst fail of my short life so far. I'm sure you'll agree that there's quite a lot of competition for the top spot...

Last September I was walking to school and found a massive, prickly conker that had fallen from a tree. I carefully trod on the edge of it and the case split open and out popped a huge, shiny conker. It was the biggest conker I had ever seen in my whole life!

I picked it up and shoved it in my pocket. My mum was shouting at me to hurry up because we were going to be late, AGAIN!!!.

When I got into the playground I immediately declared that it was now OFFICIALLY conker season, by saying, erm, "It's officially conker season everyone!" About 4 people actually heard - Ali, Freya, Mr King and a boy a couple of years below who said, "What's honker season? Is it to do with noses?"

At playtime we planned a big tournament for the next day. Everyone was going to bring in their absolute best conker and at the end of the day we would have a champion.

I called my beast of a conker 'The Dark Destroyer' and I was pretty confident that he'd do well. But, by the time I'd got home, I kind of decided that I didn't want to risk him getting damaged. I looked online about how to make your conker stronger.

Some of the suggestions were:

1) Cook it in the oven

2) Freeze it

3) Cook it, then freeze it

4) Freeze it, then cook it

5) Varnish it

6) Soak it in vinegar

7) Talk to it

8) Throw it against a wall

9) Take it for walks

10) Play it motivational

music

I didn't really think any of these sounded like they'd work so I had to think of something else. Then it came to me. Ned's favourite thing in the world to do is to collect stones (don't ask) and he'd made a pile of them behind the sofa. One of them was perfectly round and looked just like the shape of a conker.

I grabbed some paint and started work. After not too long it was looking just like the real thing, I'd painted little highlights on it and everything. I asked Dad to drill a hole through it and then I attached some string.

The next day our tournament started and my conker was literally smashing it. Nobody could beat me (surprisingly).

I may have got a bit over excited after the 10th win in a row and I also may have run around the playground swinging the 'conker' above my head shouting,

"COME AND HAVE A GO IF YOU THINK YOU'RE HARD ENOUGH!"

Just at that moment the string must've snapped under the strain and the conker flew through the air in slow motion (not actual slow motion, just in my head). It was heading straight for the Year 3 classroom window!

You'll never guess what happened next... It flew straight through the Year 3 classroom window!

Oh, you did guess.

It made a crashing noise and the WHOLE playground just stopped and looked at the window and then to me, stood there with a dangling, swaying piece of string in my hand. I let out a little whimper and then screamed -

NOOO
OOOO

Luckily, there were no children in the classroom because they were all outside. Mr Wilson wasn't quite so lucky.

He was sat at his desk eating his snack and apparently when the stone flew through the window he jumped so high that his head nearly went through the ceiling tiles. And he spent the rest of the day covered in yoghurt and smelling of raspberries.

I got into a WHOLE LOT of trouble with Mr Carnell, our headteacher. After the slowest walk possible to get to his office, he told me that I was going to have to pay £100 for the window to be replaced!

I had never even seen £100 so how was I supposed to do that?!

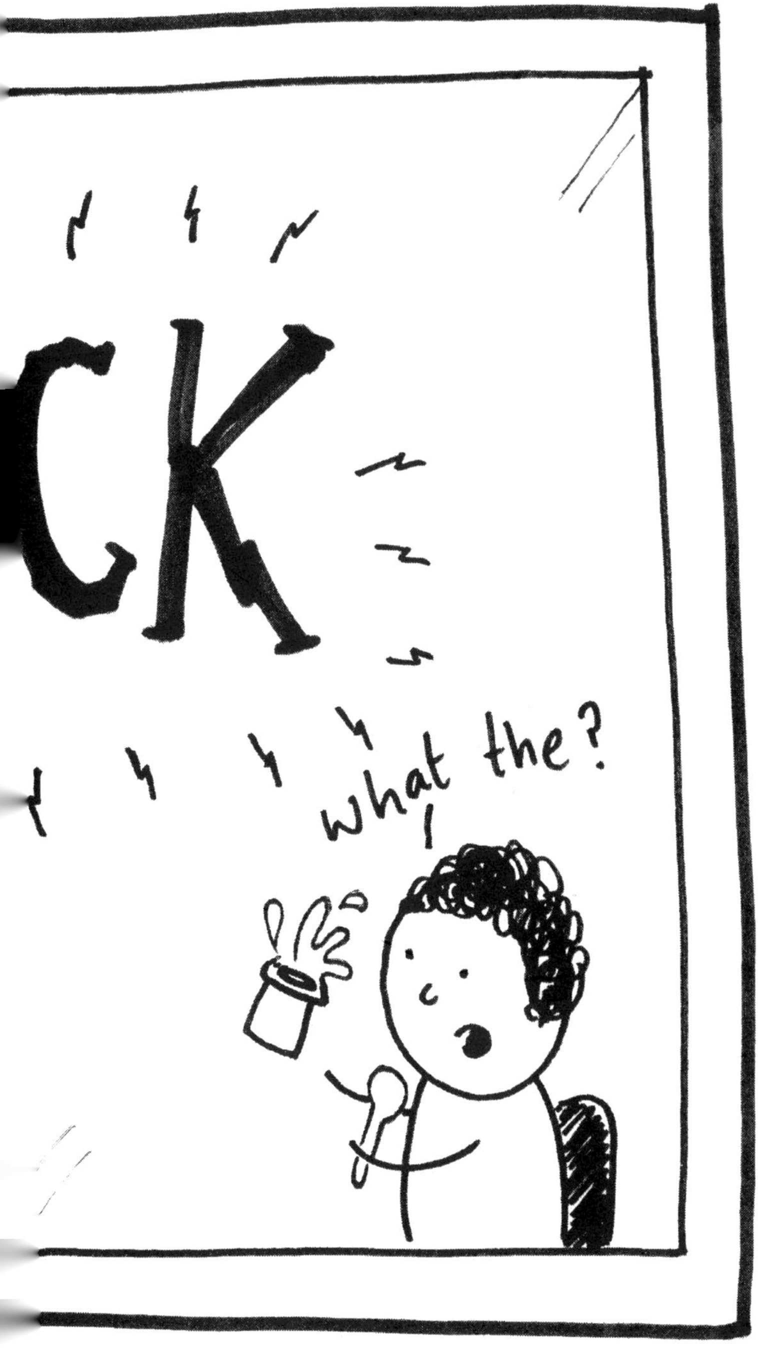
CK
what the?

To pay it off would take...

LITERALLY THE REST OF MY LIFE!

IF YOU WANT TO FIND OUT HOW I GOT ON THEN LOOK UP MY DIARY... (PTO)

PHILLIP FLOP – LIFE, LOVE, CONKERS AND ROLLER SKATING COWS.

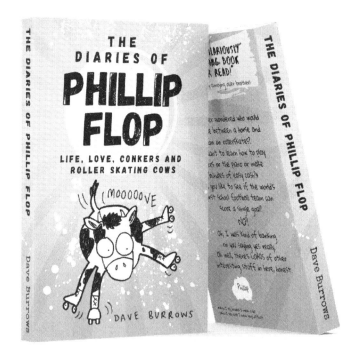

Available on Amazon

Have you ever wondered who would win a race between a horse and a cow on rollerskates?
Do you want to learn how to play conkers or the piano or make bundles of easy cash?*
Would you like to see if the world's worst school football team can score a single goal?

NO?

Oh, I was kind of banking on you saying yes really.
Oh well, there's LOADS of other interesting stuff in here, honest.

Phillip

*When I say bundles I mean a bit.
When I say easy I mean very difficult.

"Philliping great!
Mostly because I'm in it."
My dad, Nigel Flop

"I laughed so much that
a little bit of dribble
came out of my ears.
I should probably go to the
doctors about that really."
My gran, Dorothy Flop

"Woof woof woof woof woof woof woof woof. Bark."
My Dog, Ned

Translation (just in case you don't speak Dog) -

"A proper good read. So good that I didn't rip it up and eat it, like I normally do with books. Bark."

HEY YOU!

YES, YOU –
THE ONE
WITH THE
EYES AND
THE NOSE
AND
THE FACE...

IF YOU ENJOYED THIS BOOK THEN PRETTY PLEASE WITH CHERRIES* ON TOP COULD YOU LEAVE A REVIEW ON AMAZON.

*if you don't like cherries then feel free to substitute this with sprinkles and raspberry sauce, or marmite if you're weird.

ABOUT THE AUTHOR:

Dave Burrows is a new author/illustrator of humorous books for children. At the time of writing he has just sold his first book of hopefully many. (For which he wishes to thank his mum.)

His current book is the first in a series about a boy called Phillip Flop. Written in a diary format similar to Diary of a Wimpy Kid, it would appeal to fans of Jeff Kinney and David Walliams alike.

Apart from it is "obviously much better." (Thanks to his mum again.)

His favourite colour is red, his favourite word is sausages and his favourite food is, erm, sausages.

In 1992 he was awarded a certificate from the local mayor for swimming a WHOLE length of a swimming pool, something for which he is immeasurably proud, as I'm sure you would be.

Thanks for
reading!
Goodbyeeeeeee

There's
nothing more
to see here...

Seriously, why are you still turning the pages?

Are you
THAT
bored??

Go outside
and chase a
pigeon or
something.

I'm going
now.

I'm not
joking

okay, if you
insist on
hanging around

then here's a
puzzle...

Can you help Derek the Dung Beetle to find his perfect piece of poop?

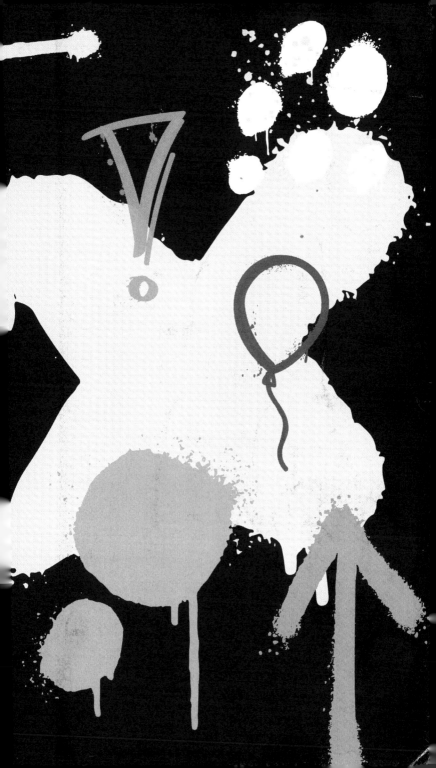

Printed in Great Britain
by Amazon

69728783R00064